McTavish:
That Rascal Squirrel

Stephen F. Austin State University Press
P.O. Box 13007, SFA Station
Nacogdoches, Texas 75962-3007
sfapress@sfasu.edu

Manufactured in the United States Of America

LIBRARY OF CONGRESS IN PUBLICATION DATA
Tollefson, Carolyn Cirullo
McTavish that Rascal Squirrel / Carolyn Cirullo Tollefson
Illustrated by: Kim Shelton

ISBN: 978-1-62288-101-7

1. Fiction. 2. Children's fiction. 3. Picture books. 4. Young readers. 5. Tollefson, Carolyn Cirullo

The paper used in this book meets the requirements of ANSI/NISO Z39.48-1992 (R 1997)
(Permanence of Paper)

McTavish:
That Rascal Squirrel

Written by
Carol Tollefson
Illustrations by
Kim Shelton

Far, far away in a mystical village with tiny houses, miniature forests, and valleys in the Glen-Coe Highlands of Scotland live the Acorn People. The villagers only grow to be six to eight inches tall and always wear acorn hats. Their clothing represents the Scottish plaid of their Clan, and they also wear sturdy little boots.

One fall afternoon, ten-year-old twins, Tavio and Tavin, and their eight-year-old sister, Aileana, went into the forrest to gather acorns for the Fall Festival. There is a prize awarded to the family who brings the most acorns to the Festival, and the children hope to win it.

An orphaned red squirrel known as McTavish watches hungrily as the children fill their basket.

When the children disappear into the woods to hunt for more acorns, McTavish leaps from the tree into the basket. He eats what he can and takes the rest to his nest, high in the tree.

When the children return, they are surprised and sad to see all the acorns they gathered have been stolen. McTavish is known for stealing acorns, so the children suspect he is responsible.

Tavio, Tavin, and Aileana run down the hill crying since they have nothing to show for their hard work. Soon they reach the village, and the fragrant smell of cinnamon and spices fill the street. Two freshly baked acorn pies cool in the bakery windows.

The owner of the bakery waves as he sweeps the front entry to his shop, but the children are so upset they do not notice or return his greeting.

Meanwhile, McTavish sits in his nest enjoying the acorns the children gathered.

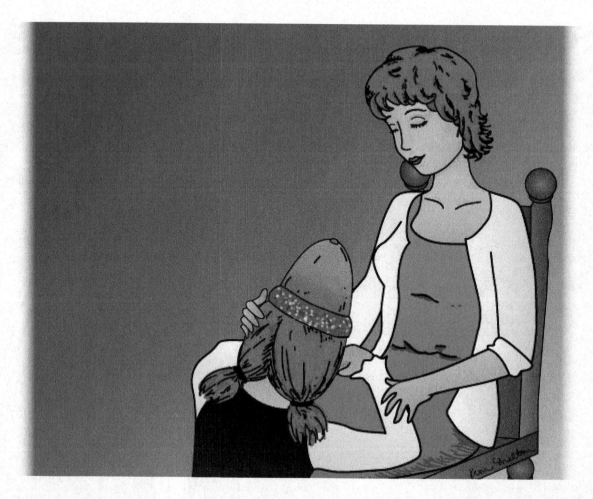

The children reach their father's bagpipe shop and rush in and explain to him what has happened. When their mother walks into the store, Aileana cries, "Oh, Mother, we worked all morning gathering acorns, but McTavish took them all."

Aileana's mother hugs her and dries her tears and reminds Aileana that McTavish is orphaned and has never learned how to gather acorns for the winter.

Welcome to the Scottish Highlands

FALL ACORN FESTIVAL

   Days later, the Fall Festival begins with a parade. Tavio and
Tavin play their bagpipes while Aileana dances to the music. A
mouse pulls the hay wagon with children inside.

Following the wagonful of children Old Man Flintheart pulls a cage with McTavish trapped inside. Flintheart drags McTavish to the town square and parks the cage. He bangs on the bars as he tells the terrified McTavish, "you will never steal acorns from me again, you rascal squirrel."

McTavish tries to hide, but there is no place to run. He doesn't understand why he is confined.

Aileana sees the frightened McTavish and begs her father to let her take him home.

"He has no mother to teach him how to gather food. We can help him, and he won't have to steal from others. He deserves a second chance," she says. Mr. and Mrs. McGregor agree.

Aileana's father looks at sad McTavish. "We will be happy to give Little McTavish a home," he says, "but Old Man Flintheart may not want to let him go."

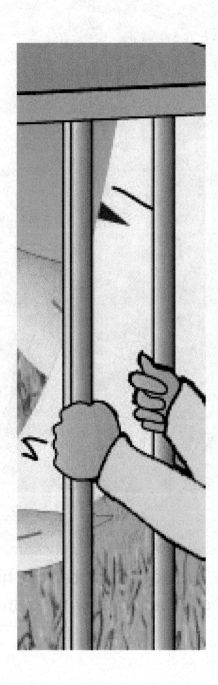

Later that day, when Mr. Flintheart fell asleep, Aileana quickly pulled the cage bars apart and freed McTavish who happily followed her home.

The children take McTavish into the woods and teach him to search for acorns and how to store them for the cold winter months ahead.

McTavish is treated with love and kindness, and so at the next Fall Festival he brings many acorns to share with the children who are his family now.